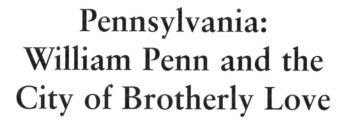

Pennsylvania:
William Penn and the
City of Brotherly Love

Mitchell Lane
PUBLISHERS

P.O. Box 196 • Hockessin, Delaware 19707

Titles in the Series

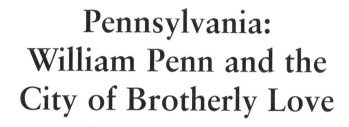

Pennsylvania:
William Penn and the
City of Brotherly Love

Bonnie Hinman

Printing   1   2   3   4   5   6   7   8   9

Library of Congress Cataloging-in-Publication Data
Hinman, Bonnie.
        Pennsylvania: William Penn and the City of Brotherly Love/by Bonnie Hinman.
        p. cm.—(Building America)
        Includes bibliographical references and index.
        ISBN 1-58415-463-2 (library bound)
        1. Penn, William, 1644-1718—Juvenile literature. 2. Pioneers—Pennsylvania—Biography—Juvenile literature. 3. Quakers—Pennsylvania—Biography—Juvenile literature. 4. Pennsylvania—History—Colonial period, ca. 1600-1775. 5. Pennsylvania—History—Revolution, 1775-1783—Juvenile literature. 6. Philadelphia (Pa.)—History—Colonia period, ca. 1600-1775—Juvenile literature. 7. Philadelphia (Pa.)—History—Revolution, 1775-1783—Juvenile literature. I. Title. II. Building America (Hockessin, Del.)
        F152.2H57 2006
        974.8'02092—dc22
                                                                                          2005036498
ISBN-10:1-58415-463-3   ISBN-13: 9781584154631

ABOUT THE AUTHOR: Bonnie Hinman, a writer for over thirty years, particularly enjoys writing about the colonial period in our country's history. William Penn played a big role in the founding of America, and Bonnie loved learning more about him. Bonnie graduated from Missouri State University and has taught creative writing at Crowder College. Her books for Mitchell Lane Publishers include *Florence Nightingale and the Advancement of Nursing* and *The Life and Times of William Penn.* Her book *A Stranger in His Own House: The Story of W.E.B. Du Bois* (Morgan Reynolds) was chosen for the 2006 New York Public Library's Books for the Teen Age. She lives in Joplin, Missouri, with her husband, Bill, two cats, and three dogs.

PHOTO CREDITS: Cover, pp. 1, 3—North Wind Picture Archives; pp. 6, 9—Getty Images; p. 13—North Wind Picture Archives; p. 14—Getty Images; p. 17—North Wind Picture Archives; p. 20—Andrea Pickens; p. 23—North Wind Picture Archives; p. 26—Getty Images; p. 29—Corbis; p.32—Library of Congress; p. 34—North Wind Picture Archives; p. 37—Getty Images; p. 39—Library of Congress

PUBLISHER'S NOTE: This story is based on the author's extensive research, which she believes to be accurate. Documentation of such research is contained on page 46.
        The internet sites referenced herein were active as of the publication date. Due to the fleeting nature of some web sites, we cannot guarantee they will all be active when you are reading this book.
                                                                                                      PLB

Contents

*For Your Information

William Penn, founder of Pennsylvania, posed for this portrait when he was middle-aged. He is dressed plainly in Quaker style and has a sober expression as befitted an upright Quaker gentleman at the end of the 17th century.

Chapter

1

The Seed of a Nation

William Penn, the founder of Pennsylvania, had his first brush with the law when he was twenty-two. He hadn't been out drinking and troublemaking as might have been expected of a young man of his class in 1667. He had been attending a meeting in Cork, Ireland.

Penn had recently been converted—or convinced, as the Quakers called it—to the Quaker faith. In September 1667 he was at a church meeting when a soldier broke into the room and created a disturbance. At that time, Quakers were the target of mistreatment by the authorities. It wasn't unusual for a soldier or constable to loudly interrupt a Quaker service, claiming the Quakers were holding a riotous gathering, and cart the whole congregation off to jail.

Penn's first reaction was to intercept the intruding soldier and throw him out of the building. The other Quakers persuaded him that physical violence was not their way to handle the situation. Penn reluctantly let the man go, but the damage had been done. The soldier reported to the local authorities that he had been attacked. Soon there were policemen at the meeting door to arrest nineteen of the Quakers, including Penn.

Penn demanded that he be treated just like his fellow Quakers, even though the mayor or magistrate wished to release him. Evidently

Penn's elaborate clothing made the mayor think he wasn't one of the Quakers, who dressed simply.

Eventually Penn was released along with the others, but it wasn't the last time he would be arrested. Seeing firsthand the persecution that Quakers had to endure only strengthened his determination to help fellow Quakers fight for religious freedom.

Each year brought new troubles for the Quakers. In 1670 the Conventicle Act went back into effect in England after it had lapsed for a time. This act was aimed at preventing Catholicism from gaining a hold in England, but Quakers took the brunt of the renewed enforcement. Parliament declared that it was illegal for any religious group to meet who didn't follow Anglican, or Church of England, beliefs.

Quakers didn't think that the Conventicle Act could legally be applied to them, so many leaders set out to test the act in court. They did this by purposefully meeting together and welcoming arrest. When arrested, they were usually fined heavily for unlawful assembly.

William Penn had recently returned to London from managing his father's estates in Ireland. He was eager to do his part in testing the Conventicle Act. Penn went to the Gracechurch Street Meeting House on August 14, 1670, to find it closed and guarded by soldiers. Penn began teaching quietly to the worshipers, who gathered on the street corner.

The constables arrived and Penn was taken to jail, along with a man named William Mead. Charged with "causing a great tumult of people on the royal street to be there gathered together riotously and rout-ously,"[1] Penn and Mead remained in custody until a trial could be held.

The trial did not go well for the Lord Mayor, who presided as judge. Penn was persuasive in his defense of Mead and himself, and skillful in his legal challenges. When the judge asked Penn to plead to his indictment, Penn asked, "Shall I plead to an indictment that hath no foundation in law? If it contain that law you say I have broken, why should you decline to produce that law, since it will be impossible for the jury to determine, or agree to bring in their verdict, who have not the law produced, by which they should measure the truth of this indictment, and the guilt, or contrary, of my fact." The judge was not pleased and called Penn "a sawcy fellow."[2]

In the end the jury was so moved by Penn's and Mead's testi-monies that they refused to convict the pair even after the Lord Mayor threatened them with jail if they didn't convict. They were locked up in the jury chambers to think things over but still refused to give the verdict that the mayor directed.

Police took the jury members away to Newgate Prison. They remained there until they paid the fines assessed by the Lord Mayor. Penn would have stayed in jail with the jury, but his father was quite sick. Penn allowed his father, Sir William, to pay the fines so that Penn could hurry to the dying man's bedside.

Eventually the highest court in England said that the jury had been illegally fined and imprisoned. The justices said that a jury could not be punished for its verdict. William Penn had brought about an important addition to the body of common law in England that had been building for centuries.

The years following this victory were full of trouble for Quakers. Even though the target of so many of the unjust laws were Catholics, Quakers suffered right alongside them. Quakers refused to take an oath of loyalty to the king because their faith didn't allow them to swear oaths. Many Quaker leaders pleaded that they would gladly give their word that they were loyal to the king, but that wasn't good enough for the authori-

Penn's father, Sir William Penn Sr., wasn't a Quaker and didn't like that his son had joined that faith. Sir William had risen from sea captain to admiral partly because he had maintained close ties to the British kings. The official religion of the Crown was the Church of England, so Sir William approved only of that church. Father and son reconciled before Sir William's death on September 16, 1670.

ties. There seemed no room for common sense in England during those days of unrest.

Even the elections were full of treachery and deceit as local and even national authorities tried to get certain candidates elected. Sometimes elections would be announced for a certain day and then hurriedly changed at the last moment to benefit the favored candidates.

During this time, William Penn worked diligently to change his country. He wrote pamphlets and worked to elect honest candidates to Parliament. He gave speeches and met with government leaders. In spite of his efforts and those of other honest men, the situation only grew worse for Quakers and other religious minorities.

At last Penn was forced to return to an old idea. Could the Quakers move to America and build a new life there? West New Jersey was already a successful Quaker colony in the New World, but its land area was small. There wasn't enough room for thousands of Quakers to settle within its boundaries. More land was needed.

Within what seemed like a very short time, Penn obtained a land grant from King Charles II. Penn would build a new home for the persecuted Quakers, who would come from England, Ireland, Germany, Holland, and throughout Europe. The king ordered that the new colony be called Pennsylvania, after Sir William Penn, who had been a good friend to the king.

The day after the grant was made official, Penn wrote to a friend in Ireland: "It is a clear and just thing, and my God that has given it me through many difficulties, will, I believe, bless and make it the seed of a nation. I shall have a tender care to the government, that it be well laid at first."[3]

William Penn had set forces in motion that certainly would create a colony that would be "the seed of a nation."

Quakers

Quakers got their name when their founder, George Fox, was sentenced to jail by an English justice of the peace in 1650. Fox told the official to "tremble at the word of the Lord."[4] The justice laughed at Fox and called him and his followers Quakers, since they evidently quaked when the Lord visited them. The name stuck. Over the years it lost the original derisive meaning.

George Fox

Quakers—or Friends, as they are also called—believe in the Bible, and part of their interpretation is that men and women are all spiritually and otherwise equal before God. They believe that all persons can experience an "inner light" from God.

They also believe that war is wrong and won't serve in armies. They dress and live simply, using the Bible as their guide. They also refuse to take formal oaths, saying that this too is against Biblical teachings.

One of the Quaker behaviors that most infuriated the English upper class in William Penn's time was their refusal to take off their hats as a sign of respect for people of a higher social class. Quakers said that all men and women were equal, and none deserves special treatment.

Quakers considered it a duty to answer any charge or question asked about their faith. Sometimes the authorities in seventeenth-century England used this habit to trap followers. When they asked a question, authorities could count on the Quakers to answer by saying something deemed illegal and then could arrest them. It wasn't that Quakers sought out confrontation. It came to them in the course of defending—or merely explaining—their faith.

Quakers remain an active religious body and maintain many of their original beliefs and practices. They are probably best known for their pacifism, which prevents them from fighting in wars.

Quaker services are sometimes long and quiet. The congregation waits for its members to be moved by the Spirit and rise to speak. In colonial times, women might tend to other duties during the meeting, such as spinning thread from wool.

Chapter

2

The Holy Experiment

William Penn's family had not been happy when the young man declared his conversion to the Quaker faith. Penn's father, Sir William, had been important in government circles for many years. He started out as a sea captain but rose to become an admiral in the British Navy. He had maintained his loyalty to the Stuart kings through the English civil wars and the rule of Oliver Cromwell. Quakers were considered troublemakers by the kings, and were not much more highly regarded by Parliament.

Sir William had not educated his intelligent son only to see him cast his lot with the Quakers. William the son was determined to do just that. There was trouble between the two for years, although young Penn seems always to have been respectful to his father. In the end it was the father who gave in. Father and son made up before Sir William died in 1670.

Eleven years later, Penn received the charter for Pennsylvania largely as a result of his father's friendship with King Charles II. The land grant was supposedly made in payment for a debt owed by the king to Sir William. But the king may have had other motives for suddenly deciding to repay a debt to a man who would never have expected repayment: If all went well, the king would be getting rid of a large number of troublesome Quakers. Since many of them were also Whigs, which was the opposition party to the king's followers, sending them off carried a double benefit. Whatever his motives, King Charles probably did want to honor his old friend. And he may have also wanted to keep that old friend's son out of jail.

After the charter was awarded, William Penn turned to the planning of his colony. He called the Pennsylvania Colony a "holy experiment" where people of many faiths could live together peacefully. It was to be a haven for persecuted Quakers, but other groups were welcomed.

In an early example of successful marketing, Penn advertised widely for settlers to join him in the New World. He wrote pamphlets that

William Penn received the charter of Pennsylvania from King Charles II, which made his ownership of Pennsylvania official. The final document was dated March 4, 1681. Penn had begun planning his new colony while the land grant request made its way through government offices for signatures.

praised the new land of Pennsylvania and distributed them throughout England, Scotland, Germany, and other European countries.

While Penn waited for settlers to sign up, he tended to other details such as the planning of a government. Penn called his plan the Frame of Government. With both an appointed council and an elected assembly, it was closer to a real democracy than any of the American colonies would see for some time. The governor was to be head of the council and have veto power. Legislation started in the council, but the assembly had to approve it.[1]

Freedom of religion was guaranteed, although it was just freedom to decide *which* religion to follow. All free men could vote only if they met property qualifications and said they believed in God. There was no provision for nonbelievers. The right to a jury trial was guaranteed, and only murder and treason could be punished by death.

Perhaps the most striking part of Penn's Frame of Government was the provision he made for it to be amended if the need arose. He was giving away some of the power that he had rightfully been given.[2]

Penn wrote letters to the colonists who were already in Pennsylvania and to the Indians who lived there. Penn's letter to the Delaware, Susquehannock, and Shawnee Indians who lived in the area indicated an unusual attitude for the times in which he lived. He wrote, "My Friends: There is one great God and power that hath made the world and all things therein, to whom you and I must one day give an account, for all that we do in the world."[3]

Penn went on to say that he wanted to live together as neighbors and friends with the Indians. Few Europeans in the seventeenth century considered Indians to be more than savages, let alone that they were the Europeans' equals before God.

After many delays, William Penn landed in Pennsylvania in October 1682. He was greeted enthusiastically by settlers who had arrived earlier and by curious Indians from several tribes. Penn didn't linger at the mouth of the Delaware River but set off up the river to see the site for his proposed capital.

Penn had named the new city Philadelphia, which is Greek for "brotherly love." He intended for Philadelphia to be a model city with carefully planned streets and parks. London and most great European cities had many streets meandering among crowded buildings. Penn wanted wide avenues that crossed at right angles.

The site, which had been chosen by Penn's deputy, William Markham, was on a bluff overlooking the Delaware. It was dry, so there would be few disease-carrying mosquitoes, and was suitable for the heart of Penn's Holy Experiment.

When construction of the city was begun, Penn turned to colony business. He set up courts to mediate the usual disputes over boundaries and held many meetings with the settlers and Indians to iron out problems.

Philadelphia grew and the colony prospered. Quakers and other persecuted people arrived by ship to farm the fertile land or to provide other services.

After less than two years in his colony, Penn had to return to England to settle a boundary dispute with Lord Baltimore, the governor of Maryland, the colony that lay to the south of Pennsylvania. It would be fifteen years before William Penn returned to Pennsylvania.

The years William Penn remained in England were difficult for him and for his new colony. In Britain the political situation was unsettled. James II became king after his brother Charles died, but James was then overthrown. He was Catholic, and his actions to advance his faith scared Parliament. English officials sent secret communications to invite James' Protestant daughter, Mary, and her husband, William of Orange, to use military force to take the throne in England.

James II was ousted from power, placing his good friend William Penn in a dangerous position. Ruling jointly, William and Mary couldn't be sure that they could trust Penn. Penn was arrested more than once as the new rulers tried to decide which side Penn was supporting. Pennsylvania Colony itself was even taken away from Penn for a time. In the end there was no proof that Penn had tried to help James rather than support William and Mary. The Pennsylvania proprietorship was returned to its owner.

All of the maneuvering over these affairs took years to finish. Meanwhile, Penn had problems with his colony, too. The colonists wanted more freedom than Penn had given them. They wanted the assembly to initiate laws rather than just approve what the governor and council

The Welcome *brought Penn and the first group of settlers to America in October 1682. The* Welcome *sailed up the Delaware River so that Penn and the settlers could get a better look at their new land. The colonists came ashore in several places, but their final stop was at Upland, which Penn renamed Chester.*

recommended. There was a great deal of arguing among the colonists, and many letters traveled back and forth across the ocean as Penn tried to govern from England.

Penn was saddened by the bitter disputes that broke out in the colony; he wanted the colony to be an example of a peaceful kingdom. He reasoned with the assembly leaders in a letter. "Cannot more friendly and private courses be taken to set matters to rights in an infant province whose steps are numbered and watched; for the love of God, me and the poor country, be not so governmentish; so noisy and open, in your disaffections."[4]

Penn returned to Pennsylvania in late fall 1699. The years had settled some of the disputes, and his coming helped calm the contentious settlers. Penn set to work to mediate arguments between council members and assemblymen. He met with other governors and with the local Indians to assure them that he still held them in great esteem. Land claim problems were presented and solved.

One of Penn's greatest triumphs came near the end of his second stay in Pennsylvania in 1701. He wrote a new constitution for the colony, called the Charter of Privileges. The Charter gave more rights to the freemen of Pennsylvania by allowing them to govern themselves with only a few checks by the governor.[5] The Charter of Privileges was hailed as a great step forward in government and remained the law of Pennsylvania until the Revolution.

Rumblings in England about putting all colonies under royal control made it necessary for William Penn to return there to protect his financial interests. It took years to get colony's affairs straightened out, and Penn also had problems with his personal business. He was just about ready to sell Pennsylvania Colony back to the Crown when he suffered a stroke in 1712. He lived for six more years in a gradual decline. Penn died on July 30, 1718, and the proprietorship of the Pennsylvania Colony passed to his wife and then to his sons.

Hannah Penn did a good job of handling Pennsylvania Colony affairs from her home in England. After Hannah's death, her sons were less able managers, but the proprietorship stayed in the Penn family until the Revolutionary War.

The Great Treaty

William Penn's most famous meeting wasn't formally recorded, but stories of it were passed down as legends among both settlers and Indians. It was the meeting he reportedly held with local Indians a few weeks after his arrival in Pennsylvania Colony. The meeting place

William Penn meeting with American Indians

was Shackamaxon, just north of the site of Philadelphia.

Penn met the Indians there under a huge elm tree that was later called the Treaty Elm. Several Indian tribes were represented, including the Lenni Lenape, Susquehannock, and Shawnee. Paintings done later of the event showed Penn standing in front of the gathered Indians. The men were in front with the younger braves behind and the women and children on the outer edges.[6]

Part of tradition says that Penn wore a blue sash over his plain Quaker clothes. This would have indicated his understanding that the highest ranking chieftain of his people would wear something distinctive to show rank and to show respect for the Indians.

Later stories said that an agreement was signed by Penn and the Indians, which was called the Great Treaty. There's little evidence that an actual treaty was signed that day. Indians preferred to spend much time in discussion among themselves before signing any agreement with settlers.

It is more likely that the gathering was a get-acquainted meeting. Penn could assure the Indians of his good regard for them and promise to deal fairly with them. He may have reminded them of the letter he sent while he was still in England.

Part of the legend of the Treaty Elm was that the Great Treaty was the only treaty ever made between whites and Indians that wasn't broken. That part of the legend is probably true, since William Penn always treated the Indians fairly. The same could not be said for other colonial leaders or even for Penn's own descendants.

FYI

For Your Information

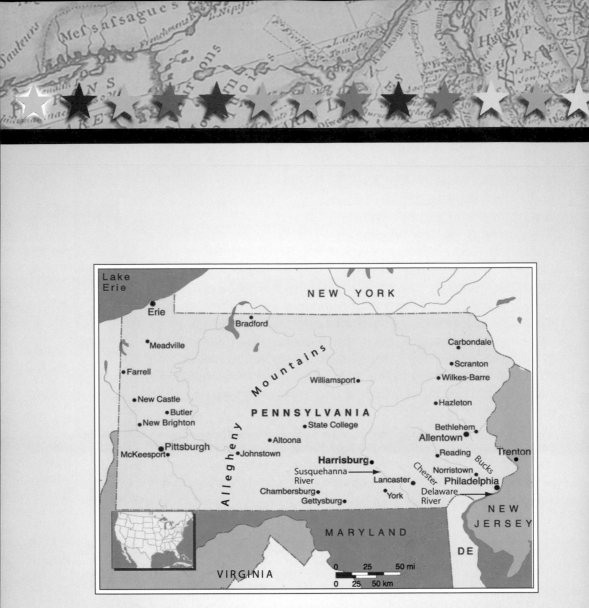

Pennsylvania colonists first settled on the Delaware River. The northern part of Delaware also belonged to Pennsylvania, giving that colony access to the Atlantic. As the colony prospered, settlements were founded farther away from the main waterways. Many of the new towns and villages were to the west of Philadelphia in the fertile land found there. Much of the land west of the Allegheny Mountains was claimed by the French.

Chapter

(3)

The Crown Jewel of the Colonies

Pennsylvania prospered in the years after William Penn's death. Huge numbers of new settlers arrived in the colony each year. Farmers found fertile land within a large semicircle around Philadelphia. There was plenty of land to farm between the coast and the Allegheny Mountains that rose in the west.

Gradually newcomers purchased land farther west of Philadelphia, and towns and villages appeared to serve the farmers. At first there were only three counties—Chester, Philadelphia, and Bucks. They all fronted on the Delaware and ran northwestward into the unsettled wilderness. As settlers moved west, the counties were subdivided and new ones were added. Counties were designed so that the courthouse that served the area would be within a dozen or so miles of any settler in the county. A farmer could do his county business without taking a long trip.[1]

Farmers were at the heart of the raw materials and finished products that steadily flowed to Philadelphia. Merchants were the backbone of the trade that made fortunes. Merchants in Philadelphia took on many roles as they organized and financed the shipping of goods back to England and other European markets. They built the warehouses that held the wheat, corn, flour, cured meat, iron, and flax until they could be loaded onto ships. Often they owned the ships, too.

Manufacturing began as well, giving the merchants pig iron to export. The iron was smelted at iron plantations in the back country and hauled to Philadelphia.

Primitive roads snaked from Philadelphia to surrounding towns like Lancaster and Chester. These roads were just 50-foot-wide strips cleared of stumps and boulders.[2] They were poor roads to start with, and increased travel only made them more rutted and precarious. Finally, in 1741, the Great Conestoga Road to Lancaster from Philadelphia was completed. It was the colony's first real attempt at interior development and improved traveling conditions on that 70-mile stretch at least.

Settlement also went north from Philadelphia, but growth in that direction depended upon Indian relations. William Penn had tried to conduct business fairly with the Delaware and other Indian tribes. He always paid for any land that was needed. The Indians were usually agreeable to selling but had a different concept of land ownership than the settlers did. In general the Indians thought they were selling mutual use of the lands, not the exclusive title that the settlers understood.[3]

In 1737, a land deal with the Indians went wrong, seriously damaging Indian relations. In later years the deal came to be called the Walking Purchase and was used as an example of how the Indians of that time were cheated by the colonists.

William Penn had negotiated for and purchased a strip of land from the Lenni Lenape or Delaware Indians that went along the Delaware River north of Philadelphia. The Indians measured their land distances in how far a man could walk in a certain number of days, rather than in miles. They sold Penn as much land as a man could walk in three days. Penn decided that a day and a half's walk, which was about 40 miles, was plenty for the colony's use at that time. He paid for but deferred taking ownership of the other day and a half's walk of land.

In 1737, Penn's son, Thomas, together with Penn's longtime business agent in Pennsylvania, James Logan, wanted to take possession of the rest of that land. Ignoring the original spirit of the sale, Penn and Logan hired three athletic men and offered a big reward for the one who could walk the farthest in 36 hours. The man who won the prize walked over 66 miles rather than the anticipated 40.

The Indians saw this as a very dishonorable way of doing business and never forgot the trickery of the white men. The deal soured Indian relations that had been mostly peaceful since the first Quakers arrived.

By the mid-eighteenth century, Philadelphia was the jewel of colonial America. Penn's plan for his city had allowed for residential and commercial growth. The wealthy merchant class grew and demanded the finer things in life—including education, medical care, cultured entertainment, and libraries.

One man became the driving force for the creation of many of these finer things. Benjamin Franklin, who was born and grew up in Boston, Massachusetts, came to Philadelphia as a young man. His amazing energy and intellect were behind dozens of the improvements Philadelphia city fathers could point to when they wanted to impress a visitor.

Franklin began his career in Philadelphia as a printer/newspaper owner and editor. In line with his printing abilities, he started

Two Delaware Indian braves supervised the completion of the Walking Purchase agreement. William Penn had purchased from the Delaware chiefs as much land as a man could walk in three days. He only took possession of a day and a half's walk at first. The other half of the land was claimed later by Penn's son, Thomas. The Delawares felt they were cheated by Thomas.

Poor Richard's Almanack, which was a collection of useful information, including long-range weather forecasts and star and moon positions. Franklin included clever sayings that have become part of American folklore. Almanacs are still popular reading material today.

With Dr. Thomas Bond as a partner, Franklin helped found the first hospital in what would become the United States. The Pennsylvania Hospital was first chartered by the colonial assembly in 1751 to care for the poor and the mentally or physically ill. Franklin used a new device for funding the hospital—the matching grant. He proposed that if individuals would give 2,000 pounds sterling, the Assembly would match that amount. Individuals and politicians found this proposal pleasing, and the hospital was soon built.[4]

Franklin also organized the first volunteer fire department and helped start the first public library. When he wasn't working at his print shop, and after he retired from that job, Franklin was an inventor and scientist.

One of his best known scientific experiments was the one that proved the existence of electricity in the air during rainstorms. With son William as his assistant, Franklin flew a kite as a thunderstorm approached. He was able to draw an electrical charge through the kite string and into a key attached to the string. With the knowledge he gained, he advised people to place iron rods on top of tall buildings to draw the lightning and discharge it harmlessly into the ground. These rods, called lightning rods, are still used today.[5]

While Franklin was busy with all his many pursuits in Philadelphia, Pennsylvania politics saw some changes. By the middle of the eighteenth century, France and Britain had been fighting over North American territory off and on for more than fifty years. In 1750, France controlled Canada and the land around the Great Lakes, while Britain had the thirteen colonies. Each wanted what the other had, and western Pennsylvania Colony became a prize worth fighting for. Britain wanted to settle the fertile land west of the Allegheny Mountains, while France wanted to dominate the area, which pleased most of the Indians in the region. If the British took over, the Indians would be pushed farther west. If a conflict were to break out, the French could easily ally with the Indians.

Iron Plantations

Iron plantations produced pig or bar iron to be used by blacksmiths or toolmakers. It was sold locally in Philadelphia and other colonies but was also a profitable export to Britain.

Molten Iron

An iron plantation needed a large supply of wood to make charcoal, a limestone quarry, and the iron ore itself. Iron smelting required that charcoal, limestone, and the ore be loaded into the top of a tall blast furnace, which was lined with brick. Air was pumped into the furnace with huge bellows, and the resulting hot fire separated the iron from the other materials. Liquid iron ran out the bottom of the furnace to be cast into pigs.

The iron workers lived in small homes near the furnace building. Their families lived with them, and all were supervised by the ironmaster, who was the local manager and usually shared ownership with Philadelphia merchants.

The iron plantation was nearly self-sufficient. The plantation produced most of its own food and some of its clothing. Flax and hemp grew in surrounding fields, as well as crops for food for people and animals. Sometimes sheep were kept for their wool.

The ironmaster lived in a big house in the center of the plantation. Unlike the primitive stone or wooden worker houses, this home had large rooms with fine furnishings. The yard was often landscaped with numerous flowers.

The workers had little time for fun, but they did sometimes attend barn dances or local farm fairs. The ironmaster often kept a pack of hounds so that he could foxhunt.

Schooling was meager and provided only for the ironmaster's children, and perhaps for a few of the better-paid workers' children. Often the plantation clerk was the teacher. There were few churches in the back country of Pennsylvania, so traveling preachers filled that need on an irregular basis.

In many ways iron plantations were like the better known Southern plantations, but the heart of these plantations was lit up with the glare of the blast furnace.

A battle scene from the French and Indian War (1754–1763) shows the kind of wooded terrain that plagued the British. They weren't used to fighting in the woods and found the backcountry of Pennsylvania an impossible field for battle.

Chapter

(4)

No Taxation Without Representation

In the 1750s, the French built several forts in western Pennsylvania to protect their fur trade with the Indians. The Virginia Colony, which also claimed part of Pennsylvania, sent a young Virginian, George Washington, to tell the French to get out. Washington delivered the message in the fall of 1753. Not unexpectedly, the French declined to leave.

The following spring Washington was sent back with 150 soldiers to build Fort Pitt near where the modern city of Pittsburgh, Pennsylvania, now stands. The troops encountered a French force intent on building their own fort, Fort Duquesne, at the same place. The first battle of the French and Indian War took place near Great Meadows, about 25 miles south of the proposed fort site on the Ohio River. Washington won the battle but was soon driven back when a much larger French force arrived.[1]

The name French and Indian War is misleading, because Indians fought on both sides. On one side were British soldiers, colonists, and some Indian allies. On the other side were the French, many more Indians, and some Canadians.

When word reached England that the French had gained control of all of western Pennsylvania, Parliament sent General Edward Braddock and a thousand soldiers to America. Braddock appointed George Washington as his aide, and the expedition set out in June 1755. They planned to capture the French Fort Duquesne.

Braddock and his British regulars were joined by hundreds of colonial troops.[2] Woodchoppers led the way as they cut a trail through absolute wilderness. Next came the fife and bugle corps and then the soldiers. This noisy parade trailed along at about three miles a day. There was no element of surprise from this expedition.

However, General Braddock didn't think he needed to surprise the French at Fort Duquesne. In the 1700s, most European generals lined up their forces opposite each other on a field and ordered them to fire upon the enemy side. The army with the most men left standing won the battle. It wasn't considered fair to make sneak attacks or fire from behind barriers.

If the French commander believed in fighting that way, he abandoned his plans when he saw how many more men the British had. He ordered an ambush on British troops while they were camped for the night. It was reported later that Braddock's men begged to be allowed to fight from behind trees, too, but the general refused and called them cowards.[3]

Washington was sent for reinforcements and later wrote of what he saw as he made his way back up the trail through a sea of wounded and dead soldiers: "The shocking scenes which presented themselves in this night's march are not to be described. The dead, the dying, the groans, lamentations, and cries along the road were enough to pierce a heart of adamant."[4]

General Braddock himself was wounded and died two days later. Just before he died he said, "We shall better know how to deal with them another time."[5] Evidently this referred to the ungentlemanly tactics employed by the French in the sneak attack.

The war dragged on for several years. A new British general, John Forbes, led an 8,000-man army across Pennsylvania to capture Fort Duquesne. The British also won a decisive battle in 1759 at Quebec, Canada.

The French signed a peace treaty in 1763, which gave Canada, western Pennsylvania Colony, and all French territory east of the Mississippi to Britain. In a separate section of the treaty, Britain received Florida from Spain. Britain emerged as the most powerful nation in the world.

The French may have surrendered, but many of the Indians kept fighting. Unlike the French, the British wouldn't sell gunpowder or ammunition to the Indians, who needed these supplies for hunting. Several Indian tribes joined in a confederacy in spring 1763. Delaware, Ottawa, Seneca, and Shawnee Indians banded together to attack Pennsylvania frontier settlements.

The resulting uprising came to be called Pontiac's War, or Pontiac's Rebellion. Pontiac, an Ottawa Indian, was one of the leaders of the attacks. That summer was a bloody one for Indians and settlers alike. Settlers fled east as the Indians burned homes and killed the residents, often scalping their victims and occasionally taking prisoners.

Chief Pontiac was a powerful speaker as well as a great warrior. He called a meeting of more than 400 chiefs and warriors and persuaded them to join him in attacking Pennsylvania settlements. Pontiac's goal was to return the frontier area to the French.

Eventually the uprising was stopped, and a British Royal Proclamation in 1763 drew a boundary line between the British colonies and the Indian lands to the west of the Appalachian Mountains, which included the Alleghenies. No settlement was to take place west of that line. The British designed the line for two purposes: They wanted to stop the expensive Indian wars, and they wanted to stop westward expansion of their colonies. Some British lawmakers thought that further expansion would threaten Britain's economic relationship with the colonies.

The boundary line decision was not popular in Pennsylvania or in any of the other colonies. Colonists considered it their right to move west if and when they wanted to. The pride that colonists had felt in helping the British win the French and Indian War dissolved into grumbling. It was yet another policy forced on the colonies that only benefited the mother country.

Britain and the thirteen American colonies had coexisted fairly peacefully for most of the 150 years that settlers had been traveling to the New World. That friendly relationship changed after the French and Indian War.

Britain had gone deeply into debt to finance the war, and now it looked as if they would have to keep a large military force permanently in the colonies. British lawmakers could see only one solution to the money crunch this would create: The colonies would have to pay for their own defense.

For many years the colonies had paid duties, a type of tax, on imported goods. Duties were used to regulate trading, or commerce between countries. They helped make sure that goods from Britain made the highest profit. Like other colonists, Pennsylvanians didn't like the idea of paying duties, but often Britain was lax about collecting the taxes. Besides, smuggling was widely accepted and seldom punished. Britain's new resolve to enforce duties and levy new ones was not popular in America.

The first of many acts passed by the British Parliament to raise money came in 1764. It came to be called the Sugar Act because its focus was on taxing molasses. Soon thereafter, there were taxes on wine, coffee, silk, and other goods.

At first Pennsylvanians supported the taxes—or at least they accepted them. Merchants in Philadelphia and in other cities needed the trade with Britain. They understood the purpose of duties to protect trade even if they didn't like to pay them.

The Stamp Act passed by Parliament in March 1765 was a different kind of tax. The law required that colonists buy a special stamp to put on every legal and business document and on newspapers, books, and advertisements. The Sugar Act struck mostly at merchants who could raise their prices to pay the duties. The Stamp Act affected everyone.

An uproar rose in the colonies. They didn't have any representatives in the Parliament but were being forced to pay taxes. The outraged activists in the colonies howled that this was taxation without representation. Philadelphian John Dickinson wrote a series of newspaper articles that came to be known as *Letters From a Farmer in Pennsylvania*. These famous letters attacked the British policies and were widely read and quoted throughout all the colonies. The level of protest that the Stamp Act caused in America seemed to surprise the British lawmakers, who quickly repealed it.

Colonists in Boston burned English proclamations to protest the Stamp Act. Bostonians often showed their feelings in noisy demonstrations. Boston was the home of many of the American radicals who strongly supported American independence.

Any joy the colonists felt over the repeal was short-lived, because the next few years brought a stream of new acts from Parliament. Each one was more restrictive than the last.

The level of unrest in the colonies rose. There were at least two views about separating from England. Radicals saw no other future for the colonies but one that was separate from England. Moderates wanted to keep the relationship with Britain but get rid of the taxes and the British Army.

Pennsylvania was in the moderate camp. Quakers were a fairly small minority of Pennsylvanians, but they were often wealthy leaders.[6] Most of them were opposed to doing anything that might lead to violence. There were also large numbers of Germans living in the country to the west of Philadelphia. They didn't get excited over British politics.

The taxes were eventually repealed except for a tax on tea, but Pennsylvanians remained deeply divided. Most hoped to keep England in line by boycotting imported goods. However, there were citizens who wanted more vigorous action against Britain.

If Pennsylvania was moderate in its feelings about Britain, Massachusetts Bay Colony was radical. Boston became the hotbed of colonial resistance.

The first incident was what Boston radical Samuel Adams called the Boston Massacre. On March 5, 1770, a group of Boston residents threw stones at some British soldiers. Someone fired a rifle, and the resulting brawl left five colonists dead.

On December 16, 1773, members of a radical Boston group called the Sons of Liberty boarded a ship in Boston Harbor and threw chests of imported tea overboard. They were protesting the tea tax. The British closed the harbor in response to what became known as the Boston Tea Party.

By 1774 it was clear to many colonial leaders that they needed to meet to talk over the numerous troubles with Britain. Philadelphia was a logical choice because of its central location and size. It was the largest city in the colonies. Word went out to the colonies to send representatives to the First Continental Congress.

John Dickinson

John Dickinson

John Dickinson was born in 1732 in Maryland but moved to Delaware as a child. Delaware was part of Pennsylvania then. With the help of an Irish tutor, Dickinson became one of the most well-educated young men in the colonies. He studied law both in Philadelphia and in London and became a successful lawyer in Philadelphia in the late 1750s.

He was elected to the Assembly of Delaware and then to the Pennsylvania Assembly in 1762. Dickinson was a delegate from Pennsylvania to the First Continental Congress and later to the Second Congress. While he opposed Britain's tactics against the colonies, Dickinson didn't think the colonies were ready to be independent from the mother country.

Dickinson was later nicknamed the Penman of the Revolution for the writing he did during this time. Together with Thomas Jefferson, he helped write the *Declaration of the Causes and Necessity of Taking Up Arms.* He also wrote the *Olive Branch Petition,* which was sent to King George III to propose a compromise.

Dickinson didn't want to go to war, but when the vote was called for the Declaration, Dickinson didn't vote against it. He just didn't show up. He evidently believed strongly in the right of the majority to make decisions. He couldn't vote for it but knew that the majority would.

If this behavior was hard to understand, so was Dickinson's enlistment in the Continental Army. He was one of a few Congressmen to serve in the army. Dickinson fought at the Battle of Brandywine.

In 1781 Dickinson was elected governor of Delaware. After returning to Philadelphia, he was elected and served as governor of Pennsylvania from 1782 until 1785. He was a delegate to the Constitutional Convention in 1787 and helped craft the system by which each state has two senators and representatives based on population.

The First Continental Congress met in Carpenters' Hall in Philadelphia in 1774. The Carpenters' Company built the hall in 1770 and still owns and maintains the building today. Colonial carpenters founded their guild in 1724 to help members develop architectural skills and to aid their families in times of need.

Chapter

A Union Forged

The First Continental Congress convened in Carpenters' Hall on September 5, 1774. Twelve colonies sent a total of 56 delegates. Pennsylvania had seven delegates.[1]

Delegate John Morton came from Delaware County, Pennsylvania. He worked as a land surveyor for several years before being elected to the Pennsylvania assembly in 1756. He was in favor of separation from England.

Edward Biddle was born in Philadelphia and served in the provincial army for nine years before resigning to study law. He also was elected to the state assembly and was serving there when he was chosen as a delegate to the First Congress.

Charles Humphrey, a Quaker, was opposed to war with England. He had worked in milling and been a member of the state assembly. Later he voted against the Declaration of Independence.

Thomas Mifflin was also a Quaker, but he was much opposed to the British actions against the colony. Along with John Dickinson, he was one of the few Congressional delegates to take up arms against the British. For this offense he was disowned from the Society of Quakers.

Joseph Galloway, a good friend of Benjamin Franklin's, was a distinguished lawyer in Philadelphia. He went to the First Continental Congress hoping to persuade the other delegates to avoid a break with Britain. He wanted some sort of compromise government. His plan was rejected, and when war came, he sided with the British. He moved to Britain in 1778 and spent the rest of his life there.

Like many of the other delegates, George Ross was a lawyer. During his early years he was a Tory, meaning he was loyal to Britain. His politics changed and he became a staunch supporter of independence for the colonies. He was also a delegate to the Second Continental Congress and signed the Declaration of Independence.

John Dickinson, the seventh Pennsylvania delegate, was already well known for his writing about treacherous British policies. He would also be a delegate to the Second Congress.

The First Continental Congress brought little talk of revolution. Most of the delegates wanted Britain to be fairer with the colonies and agree to some kind of self-rule. After meeting for two months, the Congress adjourned. They sent petitions to Parliament asking for better treatment and planned a boycott of British products. In spite of the delegates' opposition to revolution, they advised the colonies to form militia units to defend themselves if war did come. They agreed to meet again in the spring.

Three weeks before the Second Continental Congress could open in Philadelphia on May 10, 1775, many of the delegates' opinions changed with the Battles of Lexington and Concord.

British General Thomas Gage had set out from Boston to seize gunpowder and try to catch radical leaders Samuel Adams and John Hancock. Paul Revere spread the word with his famous ride that the British were coming. The Patriots gathered at Lexington to face the British troops. It was never known who fired the first shot, but a skirmish followed and out of 75 Americans, 8 were killed.

Unlike Lexington, the Battle of Concord was an American victory. The Patriots harassed the British troops all the way back to Boston as they fired from behind trees and walls. News of this first victory spread quickly throughout the colonies. In Philadelphia the Liberty Bell pealed to announce the two battles.

Paul Revere's famous night ride took him from Boston to Lexington and halfway to Concord, where he was captured by British soldiers. The British soon released him but kept his horse. Revere went back to Lexington on foot, where he witnessed the first shots fired there on the town common.

Benjamin Franklin was a Pennsylvania delegate to the Second Continental Congress. He had been in England during the First Congress, where he had tried to influence Parliament's policy toward the colonies. At first Franklin and many of the other delegates still hoped to repair relations with Britain. In spite of those feelings, the Congress proceeded with plans for war.

The Congress appointed George Washington to be the commander of the colonial forces. Washington was reluctant at first but did accept the post of Commander of the American Army on June 16, 1775.

The day after Washington accepted his new job, the Battle of Bunker Hill took place near Boston. The British took the hill and thus the battle, but they suffered heavy losses. It was the first major battle of the American Revolution.

By fall 1775, King George had rejected any offer to compromise with his rebellious colonies. This refusal to even talk about a settlement convinced many of the delegates still meeting in Philadelphia that there was little hope of making up with Britain.

As the months went by, the delegates were given more and more disturbing news from England. The Congress learned that King George had hired German soldiers to fight in the colonies and that he was encouraging slave revolts in the South. British warships were already bombarding coastal towns, and British military leaders tried to incite Indian attacks on the western frontier of Pennsylvania and the other colonies.

By summer 1776, the debate in the Second Continental Congress was almost as hot as the chambers of the Pennsylvania State House where they met. At last a committee was appointed to draft a declaration of independence. Benjamin Franklin served, as did John Adams, Robert Livingston, and Thomas Jefferson.

No record of the committee's meetings was kept, but the end result was the Declaration of Independence, penned by Thomas Jefferson. Franklin was suffering from a severe attack of gout at the time, but he edited Jefferson's first draft, making notes and suggesting changes.[2]

When debate resumed in the Congress after a recess, John Dickinson again rose to speak passionately against declaring for independence. John Adams wrote later of Dickinson on that day: "He had prepared himself apparently with great labor and ardent zeal, and in a speech of great length, and all his eloquence, he combined together all that had before been written in pamphlets and newspapers. . . ."[3] The delegates listened carefully, but most could no longer agree with Dickinson that delay was appropriate. The vote was called and the yeas won.

Soon the bells rang all over the city and word spread across the colonies. The Declaration made the struggle official, but the war had already been under way for over a year.

In late September 1777, the British occupied Philadelphia. The Second Continental Congress was still meeting there, but news of the approaching British army convinced them to pack up and move out of town. They met at Lancaster and then at York, Pennsylvania.

Washington wanted to take Philadelphia back, but first he needed winter quarters for his army. He settled on a high plateau about 18 miles from Philadelphia. Called Valley Forge, the area offered relative safety from enemy attack and was close enough to Philadelphia for Washington to keep an eye on the British occupiers.

Winter that year was no colder or wetter than a normal Pennsylvania winter, but the soldiers staying at Valley Forge found it almost unendurable. They didn't have adequate clothing, food, or shelter. The army of 11,000 arrived at Valley Forge on December 19, 1777, at nightfall. Tents were pitched, but many men didn't have blankets or food.

By December 21, conditions were so bad that Washington wrote to Congress that "unless some great and capital change takes place . . . this Army must inevitably . . . starve, dissolve, or disperse."[4]

Washington lived in a tent at first because he had promised his soldiers to "share in the hardships and partake of every inconvenience."[5] Eventually he moved into a farmhouse, which he rented

General George Washington inspects the few troops that were able to drill during the long winter in Valley Forge. Horses suffered, too, as food for the animals became harder and harder to get. Most soldiers had far less adequate clothing than is pictured here.

from Isaac Potts. The current tenant, the widow Mrs. Deborah Hewes, moved in with her family.

By then most of the soldiers had been housed in wooden huts that they built themselves. The primitive structures were better than tents but not by much.

Washington intended to feed his troops by buying food from the farmers who lived near Valley Forge. Those supplies were soon exhausted, and transporting food any distance was extremely hard given the poor roads. Also, the distribution system that the Continental Army officials used wasn't able to get the job done.[6]

Clothing was as scarce as food. The soldiers' clothing was wearing out, and there wasn't any new to replace the old. By the beginning of February, almost 4,000 soldiers were unavailable for duty because they lacked clothes or shoes.[7]

Smallpox sickened thousands of soldiers, mostly as an aftereffect of the inoculation procedure used, which caused a mild case of smallpox in order to give immunity. (A safer inoculation, using cowpox, wouldn't be ready for almost twenty years.) Other illnesses such as pneumonia, dysentery, typhoid, and typhus were widespread. The sickest soldiers were sent to hospitals set up in nearby towns, but conditions at those hospitals were only slightly better than in the camp. It has been estimated that as many as 3,000 of the 11,000 soldiers who arrived at Valley Forge in December died before spring.

Supplies began to flow again in the spring, and conditions improved at Valley Forge. German volunteer Friedrich von Steuben arrived to teach the untrained soldiers the proper way to drill and to fight. The best news was that France was joining with the colonies against the British. Ben Franklin had gone to France to persuade them that recognizing America as an independent nation was good for both countries. He succeeded, and France signed a treaty with the Continental Congress on May 4, 1778.

By June the British decided to pull out of Philadelphia. The French decision to join the Americans convinced the British that their forces were too spread out. They packed up and boarded ships to travel north to New York. No shots were fired, but Philadelphia was freed.[8]

The war ground on with battles wins for both sides. Over the next two years, battles were fought at Monmouth, Camden, King Mountain, and Cowpens. Gradually the British began to lose ground that they had taken earlier. Eventually the French navy arrived to provide additional help for the colonists.

The last real battle of the war happened at Yorktown, Virginia, in the fall of 1781. American and French troops surrounded Yorktown, where the British under General Cornwallis were holed up. Soon after the French navy blocked an escape by sea, Cornwallis called for surrender talks on October 17. Tradition says that some British musicians played "The World Turned Upside Down" as the formal surrender took place on the afternoon of October 19. Cornwallis surrendered 7,241 men.

Small skirmishes continued off and on for many months. Washington himself continued to plan future battles, but slowly it became apparent that the British had lost their desire to hang on to their American colonies.

Peace talks began in Paris, with Benjamin Franklin in attendance. He and other colonial leaders John Jay and John Adams negotiated the treaty. It was signed in Paris on September 3, 1783. King George III presented the treaty to Parliament in December. Britain had done the unthinkable. It had given up its prized colonies.

Pennsylvania and the other colonies had forged a union. They had different backgrounds, needs, and desires, but those were put aside in the quest for freedom. Now they could call themselves the United States of America. William Penn's "Holy Experiment" had proved a successful one as Pennsylvania took its place among the thirteen liberty-loving new states. Penn's Quaker beliefs of equality and freedom of religion live on today in Pennsylvania and in every other state in the Union.

The Liberty Bell

The Pennsylvania Assembly was adding a new tower to the State House and decided it needed a bell. They ordered the Liberty Bell from England in 1751. Some historians think that the bell was supposed to commemorate the fiftieth anniversary of William Penn's 1701 Charter of Privileges, but no firm record exists of that intent.

The Liberty Bell

The bell arrived from England in late summer of 1752. The 2,000-pound bell was made of mostly copper and tin, and the circumference around the lip of the bell was 12 feet. The bell cracked the first time it was rung. Philadelphia ironworkers recast the damaged bell, and it was placed in the State House Tower. The bell rang on many occasions throughout the years, including after the first public reading of the Declaration of Independence on July 8, 1776.

Many different stories are told of when the bell cracked. Some think it cracked while ringing to celebrate George Washington's birthday in 1832, while others insist that the crack happened in 1835 when it tolled during the funeral procession of Supreme Court Chief Justice John Marshall. However, newspaper reports of the time made no mention of the bell's cracking.

In 1846, the *Philadelphia Public Ledger* reported that the bell had been repaired and rung to commemorate Washington's birthday again. That account indicates that the bell was already cracked in 1846. The paper also reported that the bell sounded clear and loud until noon when it suddenly cracked again in the zigzag pattern that we can see today.

The Liberty Bell has not rung since 1846, but it has been tapped with a mallet a few times. It was tapped in 1926 to celebrate the 150th anniversary of independence and in June 1944 in honor of D-Day.

In 2003 the Liberty Bell Center opened in Philadelphia. Visitors can view the famous bell there and see many other historical exhibits that relate to the bell.[9]

Chapter Notes

Chapter 1
The Seed of a Nation

1. Catherine Owens Peare, *William Penn* (Ann Arbor: The University of Michigan Press, 1956), p. 110.

2. Ibid., p. 116.

3. Ibid., p. 215.

4. Ibid., p. 70.

Chapter 2
The Holy Experiment

1. The Frame of Government, http://www.yale.edu/lawweb/Avalon/states/pa04.htm

2. Catherine Owens Peare, *William Penn* (Ann Arbor: The University of Michigan Press, 1956), pp. 228–229.

3. Ibid., p. 223.

4. Ibid., p. 293.

5. Ibid., pp. 381–382.

6. Hand Colored Engraving by John Hall, Penn State University Digital Library Collections.

Chapter 3
The Crown Jewel of the Colonies

1. Thomas C. Cochran, *Pennsylvania* (New York: W.W. Norton & Company, Inc., 1978), p. 11.

2. Ibid., p. 16.

3. Ibid., p. 17.

4. Esmond Wright, *Franklin of Philadelphia* (Cambridge: Harvard University Press, 1986), p. 73.

5. Walter Isaacson, *Benjamin Franklin, An American Life* (New York: Simon & Schuster, 2003), pp 140–143.

Chapter 4
No Taxation Without Representation

1. John E. Ferling, *The First of Men; A Life of George Washington* (Knoxville: The University of Tennessee Press, 1988), p. 25.

2. Thomas Lewis, *For King and Country, the Maturing of George Washington, 1748–1760* (New York: HarperCollins Publishers, 1993), p. 166.

3. Ibid., pp. 184–185.

4. Ibid., pp. 188–189.

5. Ibid., p. 189.

6. Thomas C. Cochran, *Pennsylvania* (New York: W.W. Norton & Company, Inc., 1978), p. 33.

Chapter 5
A Union Forged

1. Thomas C. Cochran, *Pennsylvania* (New York: W.W. Norton & Company, Inc., 1978), p. 36.

2. Page Talbott, editor, *Benjamin Franklin; In Search of a Better World* (New Haven and London: Yale University Press, 2005), p. 219, fig. 6.17.

3. Henry Steele Commager & Richard B. Morris, editors, *The Spirit of 'Seventy-Six'* (New York: Harper & Row, Publishers, 1958), p. 309.

4. John B. Trussell, Jr., *Birthplace of an Army; A Study of the Valley Forge Encampment* (Harrisburg: Pennsylvania Historical and Museum Commission, 1976), p. 17.

5. Ibid., p. 18.

6. Ibid., p. 33.

7. Ibid., p. 29.

8. Commager & Morris, p. 656.

9. Independence Hall Association, "Liberty Bell Timeline," http://ushistory.org/libertybell/timeline.html

Chronology

1681	William Penn receives Pennsylvania as a land grant.
1682	Penn arrives in Pennsylvania; Philadelphia is founded.
1684	Penn returns to England to settle boundary dispute with Maryland.
1699	Penn comes back to Pennsylvania for a two-year stay.
1701	Penn writes new constitution called Charter of Privileges.
1718	Penn dies in England.
1737	Thomas Penn and James Logan dishonorably conclude the Walking Purchase with Delaware Indians, souring relations between Pennsylvania settlers and Indians.
1751	The first American hospital is founded in Philadelphia.
1754	George Washington and troops win first battle of the French and Indian War at Great Meadows, south of Fort Duquesne in western Pennsylvania.
1755	American and British forces are defeated at the Battle of the Wilderness in southwestern Pennsylvania.
1763	Peace treaty is signed, ending French and Indian War, with British victorious. Pontiac's War pits Indians against frontier forts and settlers.
1774	The First Continental Congress meets in Carpenters' Hall in Philadelphia.
1775	The Second Continental Congress meets in Pennsylvania State House in Philadelphia.
1776	Declaration of Independence is approved and signed.
1777	Philadelphia is occupied by the British; Washington winters his troops at Valley Forge.
1778	The British abandon Philadelphia and head for New York.
1783	Benjamin Franklin helps negotiate the Peace Treaty of Paris, which officially ends the war and gives the colonies their independence.

Timeline in History

1620	The Puritans arrive at Plymouth, Massachusetts.
1626	Lenni Lenape sell Manhattan Island to the Dutch for $24.
1631	Mount Vesuvius erupts in Italy, killing 4,000 people.
1638	First library in the colonies is founded at Harvard.
1643	Swedish settlers begin settling Pennsylvania.
1667	A French doctor performs the first blood transfusion.
1682	Halley's comet is first described as periodic and named by Edmund Halley.
1689	Russia begins taxing men's beards.
1692	Witchcraft trials take place in Salem, Massachusetts.
1704	The first successful colonial newspaper begins publication in Boston.
1714	Champagne is invented in France.
1760	Roller skates are invented in Belgium.
1765	The Stamp Act is passed, angering the colonists, and is repealed the next year.
1770	The "Boston Massacre" leaves five Americans dead.
1773	The Boston Tea Party is held to show colonists' displeasure with the tea tax.
1775	The Revolutionary War begins at Lexington and Concord.
1778	France joins the colonists against Britain.
1781	British General Cornwallis surrenders at Yorktown, Virginia.
1783	A peace treaty is signed in Paris.
1787	Delaware become the first state by approving the Constitution.
1789	George Washington becomes first president of United States.
1796	Edward Jenner gives the first smallpox vaccination using cowpox in England.
1799	New York State abolishes slavery.
1800	The White House is completed.
1803	Louisiana Purchase is concluded.

Further Reading

For Young Readers

Anderson, Dale. *The American Revolution.* Austin, Texas: Raintree Steck-Vaughn Publishers, 2003.

Fradin, Dennis. *The Pennsylvania Colony.* Chicago: Children's Press, 1988.

Freedman, Russell. *Give Me Liberty! The Story of the Declaration of Independence.* New York: Holiday House, 2000.

Fritz, Jean. *What's the Big Idea, Ben Franklin.* New York: Scholastic, 1976,1988.

Heinrichs, Ann. *Pennsylvania.* New York: Children's Press, 2000.

Kent, Deborah. *The American Revolution, "Give Me Liberty, or Give Me Death!"* Hillside, New Jersey: Enslow Publishers, Inc., 1994.

Maestro, Betsy. *Struggle for a Continent, the French and Indian Wars, 1689-1763.* New York: HarperCollins Publishers, 2000.

Marrin, Albert. *George Washington & the Founding of a Nation.* New York: Dutton Children's Books, 2001.

Works Consulted

Baltzell, E. Digby. *Puritan Boston and Quaker Philadelphia.* New York: The Free Press, 1979.

Bobrick, Benson. *Angel in the Whirlwind: The Triumph of the American Revolution.* New York: Simon & Schuster, 1997.

Bronner, Edwin. *William Penn's "Holy Experiment."* New York: Temple University Publications, 1962.

Cochran, Thomas C. *Pennsylvania, a Bicentennial History.* New York: W.W. Norton & Co., Inc.,1978.

Commager, Henry, and Richard Morris, editors. *The Spirit of 'Seventy-Six.* New York: Harper & Row, 1975.

Ferling, John. *The First of Men; a Life of George Washington.* Knoxville: The University of Tennessee Press, 1988.

Garber, John Palmer. *The Valley of the Delaware.* Port Washington: Ira J. Friedman, Inc., 1934.

Isaacson, Walter. *Benjamin Franklin; An American Life.* New York: Simon & Schuster, 2003.

Jensen, Merrill, editor. *Tracts of the American Revolution, 1763-1776.* Indianapolis: The Bobbs-Merrill Company, Inc., 1967.

Keith, Charles. *Chronicles of Pennsylvania, Volumes One, Two, and Three.* Port Washington: Ira J. Friedman, Inc., 1917, 1969.

Lewis, Thomas. *For King and Country, the Maturing of George Washington, 1748-1760.* New York: HarperCollins Publishers, 1993.

Maier, Pauline. *American Scripture.* New York: Alfred A. Knopf, 1997.

Miller, Randall, & William Pencak, editors. *Pennsylvania, a History of the Commonwealth.* University Park, Pennsylvania: The Pennsylvania State University Press, 2002.

Morgan, Edmund. *Benjamin Franklin.* New Haven: Yale University Press, 2002.

Peare, Catherine Owens. *William Penn.* Ann Arbor: The University of Michigan Press, 1956.

Schwartz, Sally. *"A Mixed Multitude": The Struggle for Toleration in Colonial Pennsylvania.* New York: New York University Press, 1987.

Stevens, Sylvester. *Pennsylvania, Birthplace of a Nation.* New York: Random House, 1964.

Talbott, Page, editor. *Benjamin Franklin; In Search of a Better World.* New Haven and London: Yale University Press, 2005.

Tolles, Frederick. *James Logan and the Culture of Provincial America.* Westport, Connecticut: Greenwood Press, Publishers, 1957, 1978.

Trussell, John, Jr. *Birthplace of an Army; A Study of the Valley Forge Encampment.* Harrisburg: Pennsylvania Historical and Museum Commission, 1976.

Wallace, Paul. *Pennsylvania, Seed of a Nation.* New York: Harper & Row, Publishers, 1962.

Wright, Esmond. *Franklin of Philadelphia.* Cambridge: Harvard University Press, 1986.

Wright, Esmond, editor. *The Fire of Liberty.* London: The Folio Society Limited, 1983.

Zall, Paul. *Franklin on Franklin.* Lexington: The University Press of Kentucky, 2000.

On the Internet

The Electric Ben Franklin
http://www.ushistory.org/franklin/

Forrest, Tuomi. "William Penn, Visionary Proprietor"
http://xroads.virginia.edu/~CAP/PENN/pnhome.html

The French and Indian War
http://www.frenchandindianwar250.org/

Historic Valley Forge
http://www.ushistory.org/valleyforge/indcx.html

Independence Hall Association, "Liberty Bell Timeline," http://www.ushistory.org/libertybell/timeline.html

Liberty! The American Revolution
http://www.pbs.org/ktca/liberty/index.html

National Park Service: Valley Forge
http://www.nps.gov/vafo/

Pennsylvania Historical and Museum Commission: Pennsylvania State History
http://www.phmc.state.pa.us/bah/pahist/quaker.asp?secid=31

Virtual Marching Tour of the American Revolution: The Philadelphia Campaign
http://www.ushistory.org/march/index.html

Glossary

contentious
(kon-TEN-shus)
always ready to argue or fight.

commerce
(KAH-mers)
the buying and selling of goods or services.

immigration
(ih-meh-GRAY-shen)
the act of moving into a new country.

mediate
(MEE-dee-ayt)
to act between parties to try to solve differences.

militia
(muh-LIH-shah)
groups of civilians trained as soldiers but not part of a regular army.

persecution
(pur-seh-KYOO-shun)
to oppress or harass a group of people for their looks or beliefs.

radicals
(RAA-dih-kuls)
people who support extreme social and political changes.

riotous
(RY-uh-tus)
behaving in a wild or disorderly way.

smuggling
(SMUH-gling)
to sell goods illegally.

Index